Kimberley
the Koala
Fairy

by Daisy Meadows

ORCHARD

www.rainbowmagic.co.uk

The Fairyland Palace

Meadow

Stream

Beehive

Arctic Tundra

Eucalyptus Forest

Tropical Waterfall

Wild Woods Nature Reserve

Watering Hole

Pagoda

Desert Oasis

Jack Frost's Ice Castle

To Jack Frost's Zoo

Jack Frost's Spell

I love animals, yes I do,
I want my very own private zoo!
I'll capture the animals one by one,
With fairy magic to help me on!

A koala, a tiger, an Arctic fox,
I'll keep them in cages with giant locks.
Every kind of animal will be there,
A panda, a meerkat, a honey bear.
The animals will be my property,
I'll be master of a huge menagerie!

Contents

Magic in
the Tree

"So here we are again at Wild Woods.
Maybe we'll get another badge today,"
Kirsty Tate said hopefully, smiling at her
best friend, Rachel Walker.

The girls were outside the wildlife
centre with the other junior rangers,
waiting for Becky, the head of the
Wild Woods Nature Reserve. Rachel
and Kirsty had volunteered to spend a

week of their summer holidays working at the reserve, which was near Kirsty's home, and every day Becky gave the junior rangers a job to do. If the tasks were successfully completed, they each received a badge.

"It would be *brilliant* to get another one!" Rachel exclaimed, patting her backpack proudly. The girls' hard work had already earned them four badges, and they'd pinned them to the pockets of their backpacks. "It's great to know that we're helping wildlife, and it's really fun, too."

"And helping out at Wild Woods isn't our *only* job this week," Kirsty reminded Rachel. "We're helping the Baby Animal Rescue Fairies, too!"

When the girls had arrived at Wild Woods at the beginning of the week, they'd been thrilled to discover that their old friend, Bertram the frog footman from Fairyland, was there, visiting his relatives. Bertram had invited the girls to visit the Fairyland Nature Reserve with him. The girls had had a wonderful time seeing the animals and meeting the seven Baby Animal Rescue Fairies, whose job it was to protect wildlife everywhere in the human and fairy worlds. The fairies' special magical objects were the tiny animal-shaped key rings they wore attached to their clothing.

But Jack Frost and his goblins were there, too. The Ice Lord had declared that he liked the animals so much, he wanted one of each kind for his own private zoo! When Rachel and Kirsty protested that animals weren't objects to be collected, Jack Frost ignored them. He'd used a lightning bolt of freezing magic to steal the Baby Animal Rescue Fairies' key rings, whisking them away from the fairies and handing them over to his goblins. Jack Frost had then ordered the goblins to go straight to the human world and bring him back some animals for his zoo.

Rachel and Kirsty had quickly offered to help the Baby Animal Rescue Fairies protect wildlife from Jack Frost's selfish plan. The fairies had then combined

their magic, waving their wands together
to give the girls the power to talk to
animals.

"I wonder if we'll help rescue another
baby animal today?" Rachel murmured.
"The four we've met so far have all been
so cute!"

Becky came out
of the wildlife
centre, holding a
clipboard in one
hand and a bag
of equipment
in the other.
"Morning,
everyone," she
called cheerfully.

"I have lots of
jobs for you today."

She consulted her clipboard, then smiled at Rachel and Kirsty. "OK, girls, you're first. Follow me!"

Kirsty and Rachel grabbed their backpacks and hurried after Becky into the woodland.

"This is one of our nature trails," Becky explained, as they turned down a muddy path that led through the trees. The path was strewn with leaves and

twigs. Rachel noticed that the trail was marked by wooden posts with faded yellow arrows on them pointing the way.

"As you can see, it's a bit of a mess!" Becky went on. "Today I'd like you to tidy the path for our visitors and repaint the arrows on the trail posts. I'm afraid it's a big job as there are lots of them."

"We'll do our very best," Kirsty
promised. Becky handed her a rake,
then she gave Rachel a brush and a pot
of bright yellow paint.

"See you later, girls," Becky called and
left with a wave.

Eagerly the two
friends set to work.
Kirsty raked the
leaves into piles
at the side of
the path, while
Rachel began
repainting the
arrows on the
first few trail posts.
Then, when they'd
finished, the girls moved along to the
next section of the trail, and the next.

Rachel was carefully painting yet another arrow, trying to stop the paint from dripping down the post, when the sound of high, chattering voices caught her ear. She glanced up and saw two squirrels scampering down the trunk of the tree beside her.

"Four new babies!" the father squirrel said happily. "Isn't that wonderful?"

"Wonderful!" the mother squirrel agreed. "I can't wait to take them to all our favourite places in Wild Woods."

"Hello!" Rachel called to the squirrels. "We heard you talking about your new babies. We'd *love* to see them, wouldn't we, Kirsty?"

"Oh, yes!" Kirsty replied eagerly.

The squirrels glanced proudly at each other. "They're asleep in their nest in this tree," the father squirrel explained. "We'll show you the way."

Kirsty laid her rake on the grass and Rachel put the lid on the tin of paint, balancing her wet brush on top. Then they both caught hold of the lower branches of the tree, hauling themselves upwards. The squirrels led the way.

"Be careful, Kirsty," Rachel called as they clambered higher.

"Don't wory, I'm right behind you!" Kirsty assured her.

A little way up the tree, the squirrels stopped. The girls climbed up behind them and peeped into a hollow in the middle of the tree. There, nestled in a cosy bed of leaves, lay four baby squirrels. They were cuddled up together, every one of them sound asleep.

"They're gorgeous!" Kirsty whispered.

Smiling, Rachel nodded. It was then
she unexpectedly noticed a curious
golden glow on a branch just above
the nest. Her heart pounding excitedly,
Rachel peered more closely. Perched on
the branch was a little fairy, dressed in a
pink T-shirt printed with green leaves, a
swishy blue skirt and fur ankle boots.

"Oh, it's Kimberley the Koala Fairy!"
Rachel whispered to Kirsty.

Jack Frost's Zoo

Kimberley smiled at the girls, then put her finger to her lips.

"We mustn't wake these adorable squirrels," Kimberley said in a low voice. "But, girls, I'm desperate for your help. The goblins have kidnapped a baby koala called Kiki, and taken her to Jack Frost's Ice Castle!"

23

The girls exchanged glances of dismay.

"We must rescue her!" Rachel whispered.

"Let's go to the Ice Castle right away," Kirsty added.

"I knew I could rely on you, girls!" Kimberley said, relieved. "Fluffy the squirrel has offered to help, and he's waiting for us at the Fairyland Nature Reserve, so that will be our first stop."

"Thank you for letting us see your beautiful babies," Kirsty told the squirrels as Kimberley lifted her wand.

"You're welcome," the mother squirrel replied. "Give our regards to Fluffy."

"We will!" said Rachel as they turned into fairies and Kimberley's magic whirled them away to Fairyland.

Almost instantly they arrived at the Fairyland Nature Reserve to find Fluffy waiting anxiously for them.

"Hello, girls," he called, scampering over to them. "Thank you very much for coming to help."

"We must hurry," Kimberley said anxiously. "I'm *so* worried about Kiki. Fluffy, will you lead the way?"

Fluffy nodded. He darted off, and Rachel, Kirsty and Kimberley flew after him. They followed the squirrel through Fairyland, past the red and white toadstool houses and the winding river sparkling in the sunlight.

But very soon they reached a
much darker, colder place. Snow lay
everywhere and icicles hung from the
withered, leafless trees. In the distance
the girls could see Jack Frost's Ice Castle
high on a hill, the towers looming white
against the black sky.

"Almost
there,"
Fluffy called.
He tumbled
down a snowy
slope, with the girls
and Kimberley flying
nearby, and then raced
through the frosted gates into the gardens
of the Ice Castle.

The four friends hurried past the snow-
covered pines and the topiary hedges
cut into Jack Frost shapes. Then Fluffy
stopped beside a huge sign carved into
a big block of ice. The sign said *Jack
Frost's Zoo*.

"Kiki could be in the koala enclosure,"
Kimberley said. "We'd better go and
look right away."

But at that moment they heard the
sound of an angry voice inside the zoo.

"What do you mean, you've let the
koala escape? You idiots!"

"Jack Frost!" Kimberley whispered.
"Hide!"

Fluffy, Kimberley and the girls dashed
behind the ice-block sign and crouched
down out of sight.

Kirsty peeped
around the
sign and
saw Jack
Frost storm
out of
the zoo,
his goblins
scurrying
alongside him.

"That koala is the only animal you've managed to capture for my zoo, and now she's gone!" Jack Frost roared furiously. "Give me the magical key ring immediately —" Jack Frost held out his icy fingers "and I'll go and find her myself."

The goblins glanced sheepishly at each other.

"The cute little koala liked the key ring so much, we let her play with it," one of the goblins mumbled. "And she took it with her!"

Jack Frost slapped his forehead in frustration. "Can't you do *anything* right?" he yelled.

"*He* gave it to her!" the goblin said, pointing at another one.

"No, it was him!" the second goblin

gabbled, pointing at a third.

Jack Frost stamped away towards his Ice Castle. The goblins ran after him, still arguing.

"Let's check the koala enclosure," Kirsty suggested. "We may  be able to find some clues to where Kiki's gone."

The girls and Kimberley followed Fluffy into the zoo. They flew past several empty animal enclosures until they found Kiki's. It was obvious straight away that the baby koala wasn't there, but Rachel was surprised to see that the

enclosure was decorated for a party.
There were bright green streamers and
balloons hung everywhere, and a table
laden with party food. There was a large
iced cake, a big bowl of jelly, a bowl of
ice cream and other treats.

"It looks like the goblins were throwing
a party for Kiki!" Rachel remarked.

"And look, there are paw prints in the

cake icing," Kirsty pointed out. "Kiki *was* here!"

"I think the goblins have become really fond of cute little Kiki," Kimberley said with a smile. "So they've given her things *they* like – a party, with lots of delicious food to eat. But koalas aren't goblins! What they really like to do is eat eucalyptus leaves and sleep in their mothers' pouches."

"Surely there aren't any eucalyptus trees around here?" Rachel asked.

"No, there aren't," Kimberley replied. "So poor Kiki has nothing to eat. And worst of all, koalas are used to living in a much warmer part of the world. I'm really afraid that she'll freeze!"

"We can't let that happen!" Kirsty cried, horrified.

Snow
Clue

Just then they heard more angry shouting
from the castle gardens.

"Jack Frost again!" Fluffy exclaimed.

"Let's go and see what's happened,"
said Kimberley.

The four of them hurried out of the zoo
in the direction of Jack Frost's voice. As
they drew closer, they hid behind one of
the snowy pines, then peered cautiously
around the trunk.

Jack Frost was inspecting the topiary hedges that had been shaped to look just like him. But Rachel could see that on one hedge, a bite had been taken out of Jack Frost's enormous, leafy feet, and on another hedge, a chunk had been taken from his long nose. Rachel nudged Kirsty and silently pointed this out to her.

"Who has *dared* to do this?" Jack Frost thundered while the goblins cowered

against the hedges. "Someone is taking bites out of me, and I don't like it!"
He shot the goblins a warning look. "I'm going to my room to have a royal nap," he snarled. "And you'd better find that koala before I wake up!"

Then Jack Frost stalked off.

"We must find Kiki before the goblins do, and take her back home," Kirsty whispered, as the goblins argued about where to start their search.

Suddenly a shower of snow floated down from above them. Thinking it had started snowing, Rachel glanced up at the sky.

But then she saw more snow fall from the top of one of the tall pines. At first Rachel was puzzled. Who was up there, dislodging the snow? The answer came to her in a flash.

"I think Kiki's up that pine tree!" Rachel gasped as a few more flakes of snow drifted down. "I think she's tasting leaves, trying to find some eucalyptus – that's why she took bites out of the hedges!"

"Let's fly up there right away," Kirsty urged.

Kimberley and the girls zoomed up to the top of the pine tree while Fluffy ran up the trunk.

When they reached the top, Kirsty gave a cry of excitement.

"I see bite marks on these twigs!" she exclaimed. "But where's Kiki?"

"And I can see some nibbled pinecones on the next tree, too," Fluffy added. He ran along a branch and jumped into the other tree.

Rachel, Kirsty and Kimberley joined him, but there was no sign of the baby koala.

Kimberley and the girls began flitting between the pine trees, calling Kiki's name.

Meanwhile, Fluffy jumped from tree to tree, searching too. The girls could see more bite marks and discarded leaves here and there, and so they followed Kiki's winding trail. It led them towards the tall pine tree that stood next to the top tower of the Ice Castle.

Then Kirsty's eyes widened as she spotted a shower of snowflakes falling from the tree. "There she is!" Kirsty exclaimed. She whizzed through the frosty air towards the tree. Rachel, Kimberley and Fluffy followed her.

"Kiki?" Kirsty called softly. "Kiki, where are you?" But to Kirsty's intense disappointment, when she reached the tree, Kiki wasn't there.

"Where *could* Kiki have gone?" Kirsty sighed. "We've searched all the trees now."

"Maybe Kiki climbed down to the ground while we were looking for her up here," Rachel suggested.

"I'll go and see," Fluffy said, and he scampered off down the tree trunk.

At that moment, Rachel, Kirsty and Kimberley heard a shout from an open window in the tower.

"HELP!"

"That's Jack Frost!" Kimberley declared, looking puzzled. "I wonder why he's yelling like that?"

"Let's go and see!" suggested Rachel.

Koala Chaos

Quickly Kimberley, Rachel and Kirsty flew through the open window and found themselves in Jack Frost's bedroom. To their surprise, the room was in a terrible state. Pyjamas and slippers as well as countless teddy bears were strewn around the floor. The duvet had been shredded to bits, and the pillowcases had been torn from the pillows. A giant poster of Jack Frost himself had also been ripped off the wall.

"What a mess!" Kirsty said.

"And where's Jack Frost?" Rachel
wanted to know.

The bed was empty and Jack Frost
was nowhere to be seen. A sound above
their heads made the three friends glance
upwards and there, clinging to Jack
Frost's icicle chandelier, they saw a
sweet, furry little koala.

"Oh, we've found Kiki!" Kimberley

gasped, relieved. "Poor thing, she must be freezing up there."

"Kirsty, isn't she just too cute?" Rachel exclaimed.

"She's lovely!" Kirsty agreed, staring at Kiki's big dark eyes, little black nose and gorgeous fluffy ears. The girls were charmed by the baby koala and couldn't take their eyes off her.

Then Rachel noticed that Kiki was clutching something in her paw that shimmered faintly with a magical golden glow.

"Kimberley, Kiki still has your key ring!" Rachel pointed out.

"So we've found Kiki *and* my key ring both safe and sound," Kimberley cried, smiling happily.

As they watched, Kiki began stroking the key ring gently. The baby koala was obviously entranced by it, and she didn't seem to care about the cold a bit, Rachel thought.

"Kiki must have climbed in through the bedroom window while Jack Frost was asleep," Kimberley guessed. "And then she turned everything upside down, trying to find some eucalyptus leaves!"

"Kiki, are you all right?" Rachel asked gently as the three of them hovered in the air around the ice chandelier. "You must be cold and hungry."

But Kiki didn't answer. Her shinning dark eyes were fixed on Kimberley's key

ring as she tossed it
playfully into the
air and caught
it again with
her paw.
Rachel could
see that the
baby koala
was shivering a
little, though.

"We must persuade
Kiki to climb down from the chandelier
before Jack Frost comes back,"
Kimberley told the girls anxiously. "Any
ideas?"

Kirsty glanced around the room for
inspiration. Then her eyes widened
in surprise as she noticed an icy foot
sticking out from underneath the bed.

"Jack Frost!" Kirsty exclaimed. She fluttered over to the bed and peered underneath. Jack Frost was crouched there, a look of fear on his face. "Why are you hiding?"

"No reason!" Jack Frost snapped sulkily, climbing out.

"You're not afraid of this cute baby koala, are you?" Rachel asked.

"Of course not!" Jack Frost blustered, eyeing Kiki warily. But then he suddenly yelped with fright. "Keep that other creature away from me!" he roared.

Kirsty turned and saw Fluffy peeping in through the open window.

"That's only Fluffy, and he's a very friendly squirrel," Rachel explained. "He won't hurt you."

Jack Frost scowled at her. "I demand that you catch the koala and take her back to my zoo!" he yelled. "And when you've done that, you can tidy up this dreadful mess she's made!"

"Come along, girls," Kimberley said, and the three of them flew back to the baby koala, who was still clinging to the chandelier. Jack Frost watched from a safe distance. "We'll try and persuade Kiki to come down, but we're not taking her back to the zoo, whatever Jack Frost says!" Kimberley whispered.

"Hello, Kiki," Rachel said gently. "We've come to take you home."

Kiki glanced at them excitedly when she heard the word *home*. "Back to my mummy?" she asked hopefully in a sweet, growly little voice.

Before Rachel could answer, they heard the sound of running footsteps outside the bedroom. Then the door burst open with a crash!

Pillowcase Pouch

A crowd of eager goblins rushed in, tripping over their own feet and each other's. Kirsty could see they were all carrying bags of sweets.

"We'll get the koala baby down!" shouted one of the goblins. He began jumping around under the chandelier, holding the sweets out towards Kiki. The other goblins did the same.

"Come down, little koala," another goblin called, "and we'll give you some lovely sweeties!"

Kiki peered down at the goblins but didn't move.

"Sweeties! Sweeties!" the goblins chanted loudly, waving their bags in the air.

But the baby koala ignored them and began playing with Kimberley's key ring again. The goblins looked puzzled.

"Kiki doesn't eat sweets," Kimberley explained to the goblins. "Koalas only like eucalyptus leaves."

"We don't have any of those," said one of the goblins.

"Never mind," said another. "We'll just have to eat all these sweets ourselves!"

The goblins sat down in a corner and began cramming the contents of the bags into their mouths greedily.

"I want that koala out of here NOW and back in my zoo!" Jack Frost fumed, glaring at them. "Haven't you got any other ideas?" But the goblins couldn't reply because their mouths were full of sweets.

Kirsty glanced at Kiki, still swinging gently on the chandelier. To her alarm, she saw that the little koala's eyes were closing sleepily.

"Look, Kiki's really tired," Kirsty said urgently. "If she falls asleep, we'll *never* get her down from the chandelier."

Rachel frowned, wondering what they should do. Suddenly Kimberley's words to the goblins popped into her head. *Koalas only like eucalyptus leaves...*

"Maybe we can tempt Kiki down with some eucalyptus leaves!" Rachel exclaimed. "Kimberley, could you magic some up?"

"That's a fantastic idea, Rachel!" Kimberley declared. With one swift flick of her wand, she conjured up a mist of fairy sparkles and instantly a pile of narrow, scented green leaves appeared on the floor underneath the chandelier.

"Look, Kiki," Rachel called, pointing down at the floor. "Lovely eucalyptus leaves!"

Kiki opened her eyes, looking very excited. "Hurrah!" she squeaked.

She jumped from the chandelier onto a nearby cupboard and then climbed down the cupboard to the floor, still clutching the magical key ring. Jack Frost gave a shriek of fright.

"Grab that koala!" he ordered as he slid underneath the bed again. But the goblins were enjoying their sweets too much to take any notice.

Kiki sat down and eagerly began to munch the big pile of eucalyptus leaves.

"Those leaves look horrible!" one of the goblins remarked to another as he chomped on a toffee. "I'm glad we've got sweeties instead."

"Poor Kiki's very hungry," Rachel said to Kimberley and Kirsty. "She's cold and sleepy, too. She must be missing her mum's warm, cosy pouch."

Kirsty nodded. "If we could make Kiki a bit more comfortable, she might give up Kimberley's key ring," she said thoughtfully. "I was thinking, maybe we could find her some kind of pouch to snuggle into."

"Like what?" asked Rachel.

Kirsty looked around the bedroom and her eyes lit up as she spotted a pillowcase on the floor. "That would make a perfect pouch!" she said, pointing at it.

"And to make it extra warm, we could pop some bits of Jack Frost's duvet inside," Rachel suggested, glancing down at the shreds of duvet lying around them.

"Leave my duvet alone!" Jack Frost hollered from under the bed. But Kimberley and the girls ignored him. Between them they collected bits of the duvet and stuffed them inside the pillowcase.

"Kiki," Rachel called. "We've made you a cosy pouch to snooze in!"

Kiki ate the last eucalyptus leaf, then, with a squeak of pleasure, she scampered across the room. The girls and Kimberley held the pillowcase open for her, and Kiki snuggled happily down inside it, cuddling the key ring close.

"Kiki needs something else to snuggle up with, so we can have the key ring back," Kirsty murmured.

"What about one of Jack Frost's teddies?" Rachel suggested, glancing at the teddy bears strewn around the room. "He has lots of them."

Kirsty, Rachel and Kimberley flew over to the bed and looked underneath. Jack Frost scowled at them.

"Can we give Kiki one of your teddies, please?" Kirsty asked politely.

"No way!" Jack Frost muttered.

"We'll help you tidy your room in return," Kimberley promised.

"Well, all right, then…" Jack Frost agreed reluctantly, and he handed them a tattered blue teddy that was lying under the bed next to him.

Between them Kimberley and the girls carried the teddy over to Kiki. The baby koala was almost asleep.

"Kiki, here's a teddy for you to cuddle," Kirsty whispered.

Sleepily Kiki let go of the key ring and held out her paws for the teddy. Kimberley swooped joyfully down towards her key ring, and the instant she touched it, it returned to its Fairyland size. Then she waved her wand and, in a flash, Jack Frost's room was neat and

tidy again with everything in its place.
Meanwhile Rachel and Kirsty tucked
Kiki and the teddy snugly into the pouch
together.

"Aaah!" the goblins
chorused as
Kiki fell
fast asleep.
"She's so
sweet!"

With a
snort of disgust,
Jack Frost crawled out from under the
bed. "Goblins!" he shouted, "I order you
to stop those fairies!"

Kiki Goes Home

Suddenly Fluffy the squirrel leaped
through the open window and landed
on Jack Frost's bed. With a roar of fright,
Jack Frost took to his heels and bolted
from the room.

"Fluffy, thank you for your help,"
Kimberley said gratefully. "And you too,
girls. You've all been wonderful! But
now we must take this sleepy little one
home to her mum."

"I'll see you back in Fairyland, Kimberley," said Fluffy. "Goodbye, Rachel and Kirsty, and thanks for coming to our help once again."

"Bye, Fluffy," Rachel said.

"Oh, and the squirrels in the Wild Woods and their babies send their regards!" Kirsty told him.

"I shall go and visit them very soon," Fluffy said with a smile. Then he jumped out of the open window and set off for Fairyland.

"Goodbye, little koala," the goblins called, crowding around the pouch as Kimberley waved her wand once more.

A soft mist of golden sparkles swirled around Kimberley, Kiki and the girls, taking them swiftly to the koala's homeland. When the magic fairy dust

cleared, Rachel and Kirsty saw that
they were high up in a eucalyptus
tree. The tree was part of a huge forest
overlooking the deep blue sea, and the
sun was warm overhead.

Another koala was clinging to a branch
of the tree near Kimberley and the girls,
and her face lit up when she saw them.

"You've brought my baby home!" the mother koala exclaimed happily. She hurried to Kiki and lifted her tenderly out of the pillowcase. Still holding Jack Frost's teddy, Kiki didn't wake up as her mother tucked her safely in her pouch.

"Thank you," the mother koala said gratefully. "Would you like a snack of eucalyptus leaves before you go?"

"No, thank you," Rachel said with a smile. "We must be getting home now that Kiki's back where she belongs."

"Let's go, girls," said Kimberley, raising her wand. The three of them waved goodbye to the mother koala, as once more Kimberley's fairy magic whisked them away back to Wild Woods.

When they arrived, the girls were back to their human-size. Kirsty picked up her rake and Rachel opened her paint pot.

"You helped me, so now it's my turn to help you!" Kimberley told them. A few magical sparkles produced another paintbrush so that Kirsty could help Rachel paint the last yellow arrows on the posts at the end of the trail. While they did this, Kimberley used her magic to clear the rest of the path.

As they were working, the squirrels bounded past them. "Hello," called the mother squirrel. "Our babies are awake now."

"Fluffy said he's coming to visit you," Kirsty told them, and both the squirrels looked very pleased.

Then, as the girls were finishing the last two arrows, they heard the sound of voices coming along the trail.

"Time I was gone!" Kimberley said with a smile. "You've been marvellous today, girls. Thank you again!" And she disappeared off to Fairyland.

Then Becky appeared with a group of visitors. She smiled widely when she saw the cleared path and the freshly painted posts.

"Girls, you've done a fantastic job!" Becky announced. "The trail is so tidy now, and so easy to follow."

The visitors murmured in agreement.

"Not like the trail Kiki left at the Ice Castle!" Rachel whispered to Kirsty as Becky opened her bag. Kirsty grinned at her.

"Well done, girls!" Becky said, handing them a new badge each. The two badges had pictures of yellow arrows on them.

"I'll see you back at the wildlife centre."
And she escorted the visitors away.

"What will happen at Wild Woods
tomorrow?" Kirsty asked as they pinned
the badges to their backpacks.

"Will there be another Baby Animal
Rescue Fairy who needs our help?"
Rachel wondered. "I really hope so – we
only have two more magical key rings
left to find!"

**Now it's time for Kirsty and
Rachel to help...**

Rosie the Honey Bear Fairy

Read on for a sneak peek...

"I wish it could be summer all year
round," cheered Kirsty Tate.

She straightened up from filling her
wheelbarrow and smiled at her best
friend Rachel Walker. Rachel dropped a
small trowel into her own wheelbarrow
and smiled back at Kirsty.

"Me too," she said, her cheeks pink
from all her hard work. "And I wish we
could help out at the nature reserve for
longer too. I love the animals so much!"

The girls were spending a week of
their summer holidays helping at the
Wild Woods Nature Reserve as part

of a team of junior rangers. Every day, they earned badges for their backpacks by doing special tasks. Becky, the head of the nature reserve, set the tasks. That morning, she had thought of something especially lovely for them to do together.

"I'd like you to plant shrubs along the bank of the stream," she had said. "The shrubs will attract bees and butterflies to the nature reserve. We depend on them to help keep the plants alive."

The girls had filled their wheelbarrows with pots of flowering shrubs, spades, trowels, forks and watering cans.

"We're ready, Becky!" called Kirsty.

"Right," Becky replied with a grin. "Follow me!"

Read **Rosie the Honey Bear Fairy** to find out what adventures are in store for Kirsty and Rachel!

Meet the
Baby Animal Rescue
Fairies

The Baby Animal Rescue Fairies have lost all their magical items. But luckily, Kirsty and Rachel are there to save the day and make sure all baby animals in the world are safe and sound.

www.rainbowmagicbooks.co.uk

Look out for the next sparkly
Rainbow Magic Special!

Robyn the
Christmas Party Fairy

Rachel and Kirsty are helping to organise a big Christmas party.
But Jack Frost has stolen Robyn the Christmas Party Fairy's
magical objects! The girls must help Robyn,
before the spirit of Christmas is lost forever...

Out now!

Meet the fairies, play games
and get sneak peeks at
the latest books!

www.rainbowmagicbooks.co.uk

There's fairy fun for everyone on
our wonderful website.
You'll find great activities, competitions, stories and
fairy profiles, and also a special newsletter.

Get 30% off all Rainbow Magic books at

www.rainbowmagicbooks.co.uk

Enter the code RAINBOW at the checkout.
Offer ends 31 December 2013.

Offer valid in United Kingdom and Republic of Ireland only.

Competition!

The Baby Animal Rescue Fairies have created
a special competition just for you!
In the back of each book in the series there will be
a question for you to answer.
Once you have collected all the books and all
seven answers, go online and enter the competition!

We will put all the correct entries into a draw and select
a winner to receive a special Rainbow Magic Goody Bag,
featuring lots of treats for you and your fairy friends.
The winner will also star in a new Rainbow Magic story!

**In the Sweet Fairies series,
what colour dress does Layla
the Candyfloss Fairy wear?**

— — — —

Enter online now at www.rainbowmagicbooks.co.uk

No purchase required. Only one entry per child.
Two prize draws will take place on 1st April 2014 and 2nd July 2014. Alternatively readers can
send the answer on a postcard to: Rainbow Magic, Baby Animal Rescue Fairies Competition,
Orchard Books, 338 Euston Road, London, NW1 3BH. Australian readers can write to:
Rainbow Magic, Baby Animal Rescue Fairies Competition, Hachette Children's Books,
level 17/207 Kent St, Sydney, NSW 2000. E-mail: childrens.books@hachette.com.au.
New Zealand readers should write to:
Rainbow Magic, Baby Animal Rescue Fairies Competition,
4 Whetu Place, Mairangi Bay, Auckland, NZ

Meet the
Rainbow Fairies

Also available
as an ebook

Collect the seven original Rainbow Fairies
to find out how the adventure began!

www.rainbowmagicbooks.co.uk